Contents

Chapter 1
Teammates

Everyone's eyes were on
the boy as he stepped up to take
the penalty. He glanced at his
teammates. They needed
him to score. He took
a deep breath, ran up and
chipped the ball towards
the goal. Splat! He
landed on his back as
the ball looped up and
hit the bar.

Football School

By Jenny Cox

Series Editor Deborah Lock
Project Editor Camilla Gersh
Editor Nandini Gupta
Designer Emma Hobson
Art Editor Jyotsna Julka
Managing Editor Soma B. Chowdhury
Managing Art Editor Ahlawat Gunjan
Art Director Martin Wilson
Senior Producer, Pre-production Ben Marcus
Senior DTP Designer Sachin Singh
DTP Designers Anita Yadav, Syed Md. Farhan
Picture Researcher Surya Sarangi

Reading Consultant Shirley Bickler

First published in Great Britain in 2015 by
Dorling Kindersley Limited
80 Strand, London, WC2R 0RL

Copyright © 2015 Dorling Kindersley Limited
A Penguin Random House Company
10 9 8 7 6 5 4 3 2 1
001—271678—June/2015

A CIP catalogue record for this book
is available from the British Library.
ISBN: 978-0-2411-8288-8

Printed and bound in China

The publisher would like to thank the following for
their kind permission to reproduce their photographs:
(Key: a-above; b-below/bottom; c-centre; f-far; l-left; r-right; t-top)
5 Alamy Images: DonSmith. **6–7 Getty Images:** Thomas Barwick / Digital Vision.
12 Corbis: Colorsport (crb). **Getty Images:** AFP / Stringer (clb). **13 Corbis:** Laurent Baheux /
TempSport (clb); Jerry Cooke (crb). **15 Alamy Images:** Allstar Picture Library (l).
35 Alamy Images: IS098U7WR / Image Source. **41 Getty Images:** Christian MartA-nez Kempin / E+.
43 Corbis: Dario Secen / Lumi Images. **51 Getty Images:** Norman Hollands / Photolibrary.
52 Getty Images: The Catcher Photography / Moment. **53 Getty Images:** Andersen Ross /
Digital Vision. **54–55 Getty Images:** Cade Martin / UpperCut Images.
56–57 Getty Images: Tim Macpherson / Cultura
Jacket images: Front: **Getty Images:** Image Source. Spine: **Getty Images:** Cocoon / Digital Vision.
All other images © Dorling Kindersley
For further information see: www.dkimages.com

A WORLD OF IDEAS:
SEE ALL THERE IS TO KNOW

www.dk.com

"Oh Josh!" shouted
his teammates.

"Josssshhh!"

Josh woke up with a jump.
He'd had that silly dream again.

"Josh!" his mum called. "Get up!
You can't be late for your first day
at football school!"

An hour later, Josh arrived
at Silver Studs Football School.
He had won a scholarship for
the summer holidays. Suddenly
a group of children rushed past.

"Come on!" they shouted.

Josh chased them all the way to
the training ground. The children
introduced themselves. There were

the twins, George and Harriet,
who played right and left back.
A tall boy named Manny played
in goal. Then there was Patrick
from France. He was staying with
Manny and played in defence.

A brown-haired girl shook Josh's
hand. "I'm Leona. I'm a striker."

"Me too!" said Josh.

Just then, a man wearing
a blue shirt blew a whistle.

"I'm Coach Davis and
I'm in charge! Let's start
with shooting practice."

Patrick passed the ball into
Leona's path. Leona ran onto

the ball and calmly blasted it
into the goal.

Josh was next up. Harriet passed
the ball in front of Josh. Manny
charged off his line but Josh
moved quickly.

He curled the ball around Manny
into the goal.

"Nice finish, Josh," said Coach
Davis. "Okay everyone, it's time
for a practice match."

Coach Davis split the group into two teams and the game kicked off. Twenty minutes in, Josh was fouled in the penalty area.

"Penalty!" said Coach Davis.

Josh stepped up to take the penalty. Everyone was watching. He suddenly felt really nervous. He ran up to shoot but stumbled. Thud! He miskicked the ball and fell flat onto the AstroTurf.

Manny collected the ball as it trickled towards him.

"My stupid nerves!" Josh thought.

Leona gave him a hand back up. "Don't worry. It's only your first day."

KEY PLAYERS

GOALKEEPER

The goalkeeper protects the goal and can use his or her hands to catch the ball.

AGILITY	★★★★★
TACKLING	★★
PASSING	★★★
SHOOTING	★

Positions: goalkeeper only.

DEFENDER

A defender tries to stop the opposition attacking and scoring.

AGILITY	★★
TACKLING	★★★★★
PASSING	★★★
SHOOTING	★

Positions: centre back, sweeper, fullback, winger.

The 11 players on a team are grouped into positions that play special roles during a match.

MIDFIELDER

A midfielder supports the defence and creates chances to attack.

AGILITY ★★★
TACKLING ★★★
PASSING ★★★★★
SHOOTING ★★★

Positions: centre, defensive, attacking, wide.

FORWARD

An attacker scores goals and helps the midfielders.

AGILITY ★★★
TACKLING ★★
PASSING ★★★
SHOOTING ★★★★★

Positions: centre forward, striker, second striker, outside forward, winger.

FOOTBALL BLOG

HOW THE PROS TURN PRO

- First you'll need to get spotted. Join your school's team or a local club side. Most professional clubs send scouts out to these. Scouts travel around looking for talented young players.

- Getting noticed is not just about always playing at your best. Scouts are also looking for players who get stuck in and work well with teammates.

- Between the ages of 9 and 16, selected players train several times a week and must also attend regular school. At 16, the club will decide which of its academy players can advance to its youth training scheme. This is very competitive.

- After the youth training scheme, players might move on to the reserves and then an under-21 team. Players are allowed to sign a contract at 17, but most will have to wait until they are 19.

X

HOME | BLOG | COACHING

MUST-READ

[What makes a great football stadium? Read about Wembley Stadium in London.](#)

RECENT POSTS

[Find out more about how to turn pro by reading David Beckham's amazing story, from his early days at Manchester United to becoming England captain.](#)

Chapter 2
Practice

At the end of practice, Coach Davis had some big news. "Our first match of the summer is in a week's time. We've drawn to play All-Star Academy."

Josh's new teammates booed.

"All-Star Academy are our biggest rivals," explained Manny. "They keep beating us, but they only win by playing unfairly. Their striker Scotty played for us until the All Stars poached him. The worst one is their centre back, Vinnie. He always picks on Leona."

"Shush!" said the twins. "Coach is naming his team for the match!"

"We're going to play a new formation of 4-2-3-1," said Coach Davis. "That way, we can be strong in defence but hopefully still have chances to score."

Coach Davis started to read out his team, and Josh listened for his name.

"Finally, playing up front will be..."

Josh crossed his fingers.

"Leona Meadows."

Josh's heart sank. He felt really angry with himself.

"If only I'd scored that penalty, I'd be in the starting line-up," he thought. "I've got to stop messing up!"

Josh still felt down when he awoke the next morning, but he cheered up when he saw his new mates at school.

"Joshy!" shouted Manny. "Look at what George and Harriet are doing."

The twins were messing around. George kicked the ball between Harriet's legs. "Nutmeg!" he cried.

Everyone laughed. Then Manny pulled a whistle from his pocket.

"Come on, all of you!" Manny sounded just like Coach Davis. "Give me 50 laps!"

Josh laughed. He was really starting to like his new friends.

"Stop messing about, all of you," shouted Coach Davis as he came onto the pitch. He quickly set the team to work. They dribbled, tackled and volleyed all morning. At the end of training, Josh realised Leona had not missed one shot.

"How do you still score when everyone is watching you?" asked Josh.

"I pretend I'm playing in my back garden at home," replied Leona.

Josh decided he would have to give that a try.

THE PITCH

Football is played on a flat, rectangular pitch. It can be made of real grass or artificial grass like AstroTurf.

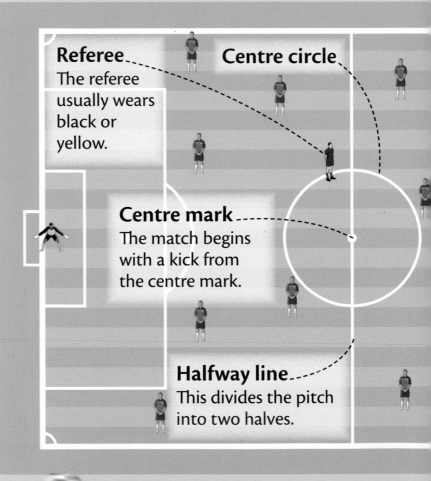

Referee
The referee usually wears black or yellow.

Centre circle

Centre mark
The match begins with a kick from the centre mark.

Halfway line
This divides the pitch into two halves.

Corner arc
Corner kicks are taken from here.

Penalty area
If a player is fouled in this box, his team will be allowed to take a penalty kick.

Goal
If the ball crosses the goal line between the goal posts, a goal is scored.

Goal area
The goalie takes goal kicks from here when the ball crosses the goal line without scoring a goal.

Penalty spot
Penalty kicks are taken from here.

FORMATIONS

4-2-3-1

In this formation, two midfielders are used in front of the defence to maintain control of the midfield and the ball. This formation provides good defence but also allows for attacking.

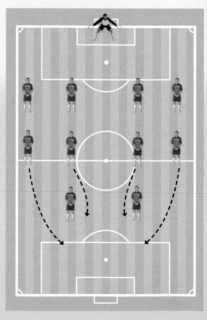

4-4-2

In a 4-4-2 formation, the two wide midfielders move up to the goal line in attack but protect the wide defenders too. This formation is good for attacking and defending.

An important part of teamwork is playing in formation. Here are some of the most common formations.

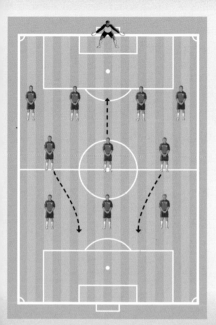

4-3-3

In this attacking formation, two midfielders push forward. The other midfielder drops back to help defence.

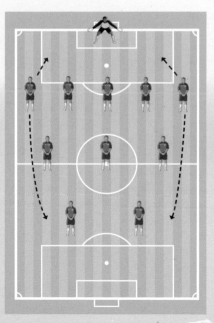

5-3-2

In this formation, the wide players (wingbacks) help with defence and attack. This formation can be very strong on defence.

Chapter 3
Match Day

Josh's alarm went off before the usual time on match day. He wanted to get an early start. Just before the game began, Josh went over to Leona.

"Good luck out there. I hope we beat them this time," he said.

"Thanks, mate," replied Leona.

The referee called Leona and Vinnie over for the coin toss.

"Heads," picked Leona.

The coin flew into the air, and Josh watched as it flipped back down.

"Please let it be heads," Josh whispered from the subs bench.

"Tails!" shouted the ref. "All-Star Academy will kick-off first."

"Let's hope our luck changes, Josh," said Coach Davis.

The All-Star Academy players seemed a lot bigger than Josh's teammates. They pushed and pulled the Studs out of the way, yet the referee did not notice. In the eleventh minute, Vinnie hit a long ball to Scotty.

"He's offside!" shouted Coach Davis. "There's no one between their player and our goalie. We should get a free kick!"

The ref refused to stop play and Scotty sprinted up the pitch. He took a shot.

"GOOOOOAAAAAAAALLLL!" yelled Scotty as he slid across the grass.

Josh could not believe it.

Silver Studs FC

The game restarted. Vinnie chased Leona down. Boom! He kicked Leona in the shin, and the ball rolled out of play.

"Ball to All-Star Academy," the ref called.

"Come on!" shouted Coach Davis. "That was a foul. It's ours!"

The referee shrugged and blew his whistle. Vinnie threw the ball back in towards Scotty. Scotty dodged past Patrick, weaved past George and then flicked the ball into the back of the net.

"This is ridiculous!" exclaimed Coach Davis.

Josh watched on from the bench feeling frustrated. The half-time whistle blew, and the two teams went back to their changing rooms.

Coach Davis gave a pep talk. "Good play out there, team. You knocked the ball about well, and our movement off the ball is good. Yes, we're 2–0 down but we can come back."

Coach turned to Leona. "Watch out for that Vinnie," he said. "He's just waiting to take you out. But whatever you do, team, don't fight back. Play fair; win fair."

Silver Studs FC

THE REFEREE

The referee has full authority during a match. He or she uses a set of official signals to show decisions made.

Advantage

Goal kick

Corner kick

Penalty kick

**Red card
(sending off)**

**Yellow card
(caution)**

**Direct
free kick**

**Indirect
free kick**

37

Chapter 4
Second Half

The Silver Studs raced back onto the field, and the second half began. The Studs quickly took control of the ball. Patrick fed the ball out wide to Harriet. Harriet passed it to Leona, and Leona ran down the wing. She skipped past

two defenders and then shot.
GOAL! It was 2–1!
  "Yes!" cried Josh, jumping up
on the bench.

After kick-off, Leona quickly picked up the ball. This time, Vinnie was waiting. Leona whipped into the penalty box. BASH! Vinnie tackled her hard.

"Arrrrgh!" cried Leona. The physio rushed on. Leona's teammates ran over. Manny was fuming.

"Idiot!" he shouted at Vinnie.

Patrick jumped in his way.

"Remember what Coach said," Patrick reminded Manny. "Play fair; win fair."

Coach Davis spoke to the physio and then returned to the bench.

"It's a nasty cut, so she needs to come off," he said. "Time to warm up, Josh!"

Silver Studs FC

Josh sprang up. He was raring to go. Then he realised what this meant. He would have to take Leona's penalty!

"I'll miss it!" panicked Josh.

His heart raced. Then he remembered Leona's tip. Josh took a deep breath. "I'm in my back garden," he thought.

He ran up and aimed for the top-left corner. The keeper

dived towards the ball but could not reach it. GOAL! Manny and the boys lifted Josh onto their shoulders. Josh could not believe it. Leona's advice had turned out to be the best footballing tip Josh had ever had.

"The Premier League will want you after that!" joked Manny.

For the rest of the match, Silver Studs were awesome. Manny made a point-blank save. Patrick cleared the ball off the goal line. The twins nutmegged Scotty.

In injury time, Josh won the ball
and backheeled it to George.
George passed it to Harriet.
Harriet crossed it up to Josh.
Josh was in the perfect position
to score. PEEP, PEEP, PEEP! The ref
blew the final whistle. The Studs
cheered. It was 2–2.

Coach Davis ran onto the pitch.
"Well done, team!"

Silver Studs FC

LEARN THE RAÍ FLICK

1 Head towards the defender with the ball and let the ball roll a bit. Then hop on the ball and grip it by the sides.

2 Jump and lift the ball with your feet behind you. Flick the ball up and over your shoulder and the defender with your heel.

46

This is a great trick for getting around defenders.

3 Run on and get ready for the ball to drop. That will be your moment to strike!

HOW TO SCORE A PENALTY

It requires nerves of steel to take a good penalty. Here is how the greats do it.

QUICKSTART GUIDE

1 PRACTISE

Practise taking penalties in an open net first. Then practise with a goalkeeper.

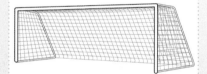

2 AIM

The corners are the hardest areas for the goalkeeper to reach. Aim for those areas.

3 MAKE A PLAN

When you are taking a penalty in a match, decide where you want to hit the kick, and stick to that plan.

4 GIVE NO CLUES

Try not to give
the goalkeeper
any clues. Aim
away from where
you are actually
going to kick.

5 CONTROL

Do not blast the ball
when you kick it.
You will have
less control over
the shot.

6 BE READY FOR A REBOUND

If the goalkeeper
saves, be ready for
any possible rebounds.
You can score even if
you miss the first shot!

Chapter 5
Victory!

"Let's celebrate!" shouted
Coach Davis. The team
changed and then headed
to the Silver Studs canteen.
Coach had organised
a big party for everyone.

"Wow!" shouted the twins.
"Burgers! Chips! Pizza!"

Manny laughed as George
and Harriet piled up their plates
with food.

Suddenly everyone started
clapping as Leona limped into
the room. She had a big bandage
on her leg, but she was still smiling.

"I knew you could do it," she said
to Josh, shaking his hand.

The next day, Josh slept in until 10 a.m. He only woke up because the phone was ringing so much.

"Josh!" called his mum. "Someone's on the phone for you!"

Josh smiled. It was probably just Manny pretending to be a scout from Man U or Spurs.

"Hello, Josh. It's Coach Swift from All-Star Academy." Josh was shocked. "We thought you played brilliantly yesterday. We want you to join us. We'll promise to play you every match."

Josh was troubled. He'd had a great week at Silver Studs. He loved his new teammates, but now All-Star Academy wanted him.

"What's up, love?" asked Josh's mum, as they sat in the garden.

He told her all about the offer.

"Well done! That's great news, but remember this: it's not about who wants you to play. It's about who you want to play for."

Josh thought for a moment, and then looked up. He knew exactly what to do.

Back at Silver Studs on Monday, the boys gathered for a training session. Coach Davis asked to speak to Josh alone.

"I heard about the offer. It's a good one. All I can say is that I'd love you to stay."

"Thanks, Coach," said Josh. "I've made my decision. I want to play for a team that plays fair and wins fair. I want to play for Silver Studs."

Coach Davis sighed with relief.

"And," added Josh, "I want to beat All-Star Academy."

Silver Studs FC

Text Message to Simon

Hi Simon! I've just made it through my 1st week at football school, and it's awesome!

Josh, that's great! What have you been doing?

Loads! Remember how I was having trouble scoring when people were watching? Well, I got some really good advice, and now I can score every time! We drew our first match against All-Star Academy, and their coach even tried to get me to join them. All-Star Academy do not play fairly, and I like all the friends I've made at Silver Studs. So I decided that I'm staying where I am.

Send

Football Quiz

1. Who is the goalkeeper for the Silver Studs?

2. How does Leona still score when everyone is watching?

3. What colours does the referee usually wear?

4. A match begins with a kick from which spot?

5. Which All-Star Academy player always picks on Leona?

Answers on page 61.

Glossary

competitive
always trying
to win

dribbling
running with the
ball and pushing it
with quick kicks

foul
when a player
breaks the rules
by kicking,
tripping or pushing
another player

nutmegging
pushing the ball
through the gap
between another
player's legs

penalty kick
shot from the
penalty spot

physio
person who helps
players recover
from injuries

scholarship
money given
for training

scout
person who looks
for talented new
players for a club

tackling
stopping the player
with the ball and
removing the ball
with the feet

volleying
kicking the ball
before it touches
the ground

Index

Answers to the Football Quiz:

1. Manny; 2. She pretends she is in her back garden at home; 3. Black or yellow; 4. Centre mark; 5. Vinnie.

Guide for Parents

DK Reads is a three-level interactive reading adventure series for children, developing the habit of reading widely for both pleasure and information. These chapter books have an exciting main narrative interspersed with a range of reading genres to suit your child's reading ability, as required by the National Curriculum. Each book is designed to develop your child's reading skills, fluency, grammar awareness, and comprehension in order to build confidence and engagement when reading.

Ready for a *Starting to Read Alone* book

YOUR CHILD SHOULD

- be able to read most words without needing to stop and break them down into sound parts.
- read smoothly, in phrases and with expression. By this level, your child will be mostly reading silently.
- self-correct when some word or sentence doesn't sound right.

A VALUABLE AND SHARED READING EXPERIENCE

For some children, text reading, particularly non-fiction, requires much effort but adult participation can make this both fun and easier. So here are a few tips on how to use this book with your child.

TIP 1 Check out the contents together before your child begins:

- invite your child to check the blurb, contents page and layout of the book and comment on it.
- ask your child to make predictions about the story.
- chat about the information your child might want to find out.

TIP 2 Encourage fluent and flexible reading:

- support your child to read in fluent, expressive phrases, making full use of punctuation and thinking about the meaning.

- encourage your child to slow down and check information where appropriate.

TIP 3 Indicators that your child is reading for meaning:

- your child will be responding to the text if he/she is self-correcting and varying his/her voice.
- your child will want to chat about what he/she is reading or is eager to turn the page to find out what will happen next.

TIP 4 Praise, share and chat:

- the factual pages tend to be more difficult than the story pages, and are designed to be shared with your child.
- encourage your child to recall specific details after each chapter.
- provide opportunities for your child to pick out interesting words and discuss what they mean.
- discuss how the author captures the reader's interest, or how effective the non-fiction layouts are.
- ask questions about the text. These help to develop comprehension skills and awareness of the language used.

A FEW ADDITIONAL TIPS

- Read to your child regularly to demonstrate fluency, phrasing and expression; to find out or check information; and for sharing enjoyment.
- Encourage your child to reread favourite texts to increase reading confidence and fluency.
- Check that your child is reading a range of different types, such as poems, jokes and following instructions.

Series consultant **Shirley Bickler** is a longtime advocate of carefully crafted, enthralling texts for young readers. Her LIFT initiative for infant teaching was the model for the National Literacy Strategy Literacy Hour, and she is co-author of ***Book Bands for Guided Reading*** published by Reading Recovery based at the Institute of Education.

Have you read these other great books from DK?

STARTING TO READ ALONE

Meet the sharks who live on the reef or come passing through.

Through Zoe's blog, discover the mysteries of the Amazon.

Embark on a mission to explore the solar system. First stop – Mars.

READING ALONE

Dramatic modern-day adventure as Mount Vesuvius re-awakens.

Time-travelling adventure caught up in the intrigue in ancient Rome.

Pulse-racing action adventure chasing twisters in Tornado Alley.

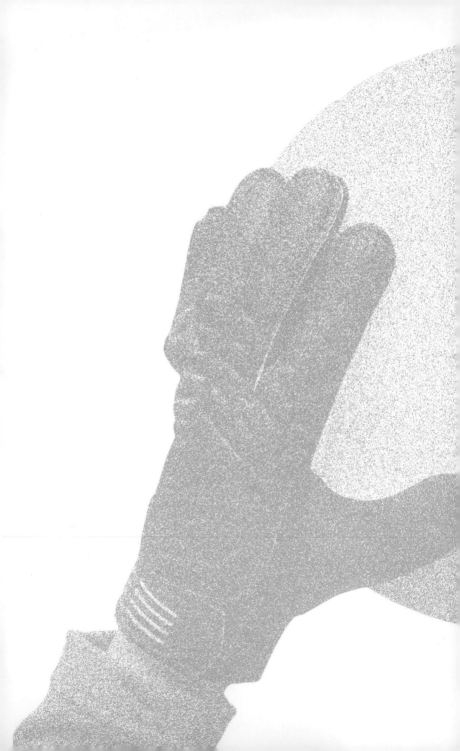